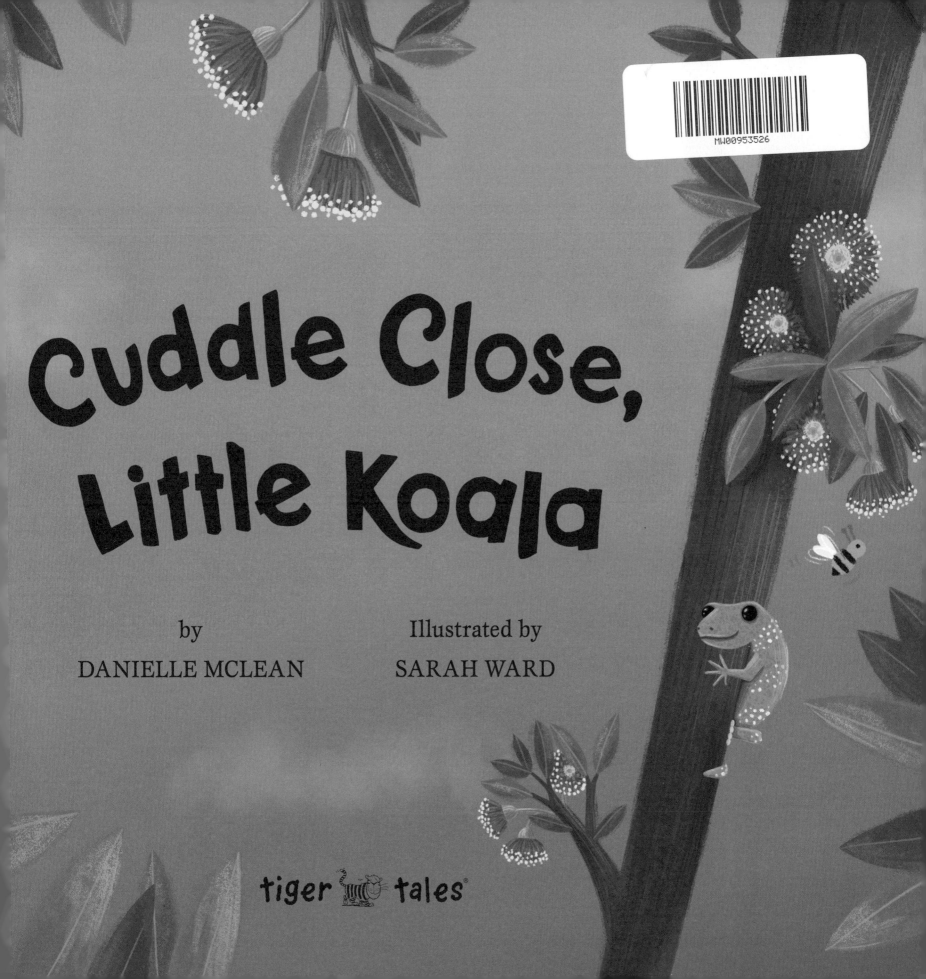

Cuddle Close, Little Koala

by
DANIELLE MCLEAN

Illustrated by
SARAH WARD

tiger tales

Up in the treetops the little koalas played,
climbing higher and higher.
"Catch me if you can,"
giggled the littlest koala to her friends.

"Five minutes until bedtime!"
called the mommy koalas
as the sun began to set.

But Little Koala couldn't see her mommy,
and she wasn't sure which way was home.
"My tree is leafy . . . and tall . . . and smells
delicious . . . ," she said.
But the trees all looked the same!

Just then, Little Koala saw
a glimpse of gray fur.
"Mommy!" she cried,
leaping toward it.

But it wasn't Mommy Koala. It was Mommy Wombat.

"You look like you need a hug," said Mommy Wombat,
and she gave Little Koala a big, wombat hug.
"Do you feel better now?"

Little Koala nodded. "Hugs are my favorite."
But what she really wanted was a hug from her mommy.

As Little Koala climbed over to the next tree, she heard
a voice telling the most exciting bedtime story.
It sounded JUST like the stories Mommy Koala told!

She rushed over, but it wasn't Mommy Koala.
It was Mommy Platypus!

"Join us for a story," Mommy Platypus said. "My babies love a bedtime tale. I bet you would, too."
"Oh, yes!" said Little Koala. "I LOVE stories."

After the story ended, she thanked Mommy Platypus
and said good night to the babies. Mommy Platypus' stories
were nice . . . but they weren't Mommy Koala's stories.
She needed to get home!

Little Koala was feeling sad when
she heard a voice singing.
It sounded JUST like her mommy!

But it wasn't Mommy Koala. It was Mommy Emu!

"Would you like a lullaby?" Mommy Emu asked.
"Yes, please," yawned Little Koala.
But Mommy Emu didn't know the right songs
—only her mommy did.

Little Koala looked around.
"Where are you, Mommy?"

Just then, Little Koala heard
something through the rustling
leaves and whispering wind . . . .

"Little Koalaa

aaaaa!"

"Mommy!" Little Koala cried, running as fast
as her paws would carry her.

Little Koala bounced into her mommy's
arms, and Mommy Koala gave her the biggest,
most perfect koala cuddle ever.
"I've had a lot of cuddles tonight, but no one
gives them like you do!" sighed Little Koala.

"And there's no one I love to cuddle more,"
replied Mommy Koala with a kiss.

And snuggled in Mommy's arms,
Little Koala settled into a deep, happy sleep.

Good night, Little Koala!